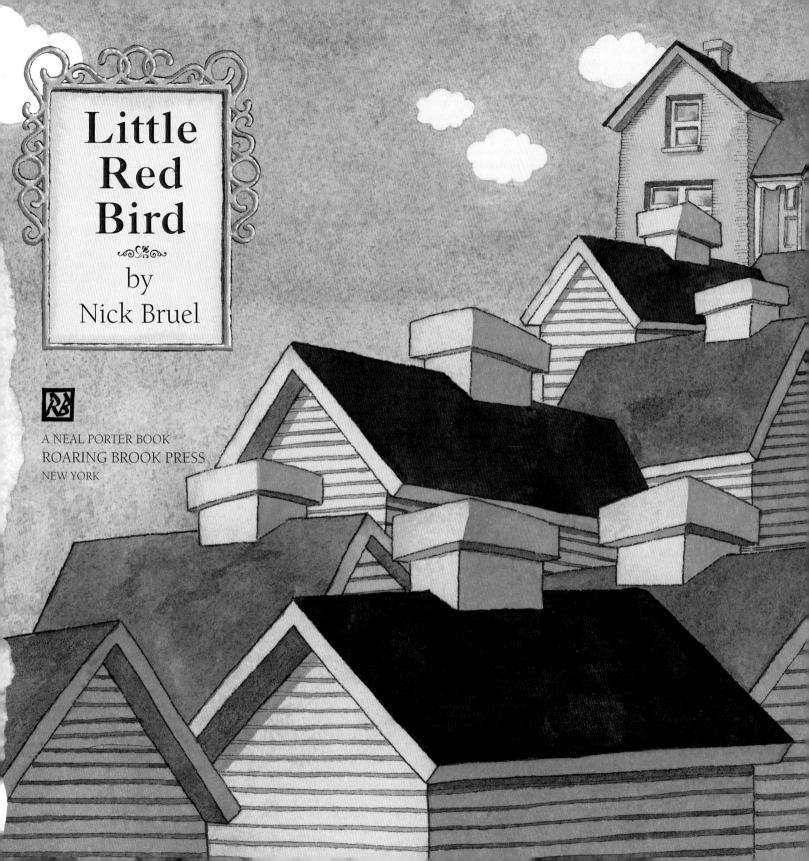

Little Red Bird

by

Nick Bruel

A NEAL PORTER BOOK
ROARING BROOK PRESS
NEW YORK

For Stephen, Aviva, Hannah and Rachel

Copyright © 2008 by Nick Bruel
A Neal Porter Book
Published by Roaring Brook Press
Roaring Brook Press is a division of Holtzbrinck Publishing Holdings Limited Partnership
175 Fifth Avenue, New York, New York 10010
All rights reserved
www.roaringbrookpress.com

Distributed in Canada by H. B. Fenn and Company, Ltd.

Library of Congress Cataloging-in-Publication Data
Bruel, Nick.
Little red bird / by Nick Bruel. — 1st ed.
p. cm.
"A Neal Porter book."
Summary: After escaping from her cage to see the world, a little red bird finds it difficult to decide
whether to stay free or to go home and never fly again.
ISBN-13: 978-1-59643-339-7   ISBN-10: 1-59643-339-6
[1. Birds—Fiction. 2. Self-confidence—Fiction. 3. Decision making—Fiction. 4. Stories in rhyme.] 1. Title.
PZ8.3.B8253Lit 2008   [E]—dc22   2007013198

Roaring Brook Press books are available for special promotions and premiums.
For details, contact: Director of Special Markets, Holtzbrinck Publishers.

Printed in China   First edition May 2008
10 9 8 7 6 5 4 3 2 1

Have you ever heard
Of the Little
Red Bird
Who lived in
a cage made
of gold?

She had
all she
could
need—

She
had
water
and seed

And
plenty to
read, I've
been told.

Have you
ever heard
Of the Little
Red Bird
Who looked out
her cage
one fine day?

Through the
curtains of lace
Was a curious
place
That looked far,
far away.

It had a sky that was blue
And green grass was there, too,
And things that she thought were
    called "trees."

Though her cage was quite neat
It was also petite.
She could not spread her wings
    with much ease.

"How could I roam
From this place
    that's my home?"
she thought to
    herself by and by.
"I have all I need
To eat, drink,
    and read . . .
But I've always
    wanted to FLY!"

Then in front of her eyes
was quite a surprise!
The door was open!
It's true!

It looked scary out there.
Should she leave?
Should she dare?
I wonder what YOU would do?

Have you ever
  heard
Of the Little
  Red Bird
Who hopped out
  of her cage
  without fear?

She hopped onto
  a rug
And said with
  a shrug,
"I could get used
  to it here."

She hopped
  onto a book.
Then
  a desk.
Then
  a hook.
Then a chair
  that was
  painted blue.

She hopped
  onto
  a bed.
Then
  a lamp
  that was red,
To have a
  better view.

"I don't mean
    to complain,
But I'm hopping
    in vain.
The room's just
    too small
    for flight.

I need a bit more....
A place where
    I'd soar.
A bigger room
    might be
    all right."

Through the curtains of lace
She saw that curious place
That looked very far, far away.

"I could never go there,"
she said with despair.
"But it might be nice if someday . . ."

Then in front of her eyes
     was quite a surprise!
The window was open! It's true!

It looked scary out there.
Should she leave? Should she dare?
I wonder what YOU would do?

Have you ever heard
Of the Little Red Bird
Who stepped out for
    the very first time?

With all of her might
She leaped into flight
Chirping . . .

The sky was so blue
As she glided
    and flew
Through the air
    with the greatest
    of ease.

She felt
    very proud
As she soared
    through a cloud

And back
    down to the
    ground on
    a breeze.

"Flying is
   the best!
Who needs a nest
Or a cage or a
   dark little room?
I'll fly here
   and there!
I'll fly everywhere!
Maybe I'll fly
   to the moon!
But before flying
   to space—
There's that
   curious place
That I had seen
   before!"
So she quickened
   her pace
And flew to
   that place
That was far, far
   away no more.

Have you
ever heard
Of the Little
Red Bird
Who flew like a
fiery spark?

Straight toward
the sun
She wouldn't
be done
Till she came
to what we call
a park.

"Everything's so green!"

"It's like nothing I've seen!"

"What's that over there?"

"Those are FLOWERS, I declare!"

"There's so much to do!"

"And the sky is so blue!"

"They call them 'trees,' I think!"

"I'm just tickled pink!"

"There's so much to discover!"

"I may never recover!"

"No cage to be kept in!"

"What have I just stepped in?"

She flew all
   afternoon
Singing a tune
About a few of
   her favorite
   things
Until finally
   she lit
On a branch
   where she'd sit
And rest
   her little
   red wings.

The sun was going down
On the small, sleepy town
That she saw in the tree
    from up high.
Night would come soon
Along with the moon
And the stars that danced
    in the sky.

"But I don't feel quite right,"
    she said at dawn's light.
"Something is missing, indeed.
I want something to drink.
    And I'm hungry, I think.
    And I wish I had
        something to read."

Then in
front of
her eyes
Was quite
a surprise!

(You'll see it when
you turn the page.)

She saw, far away,
A house that was gray.

And through the curtains of lace
A familiar place.

Inside a room that was plain
Was her former domain—

A thing made of gold,
All shiny and cold.

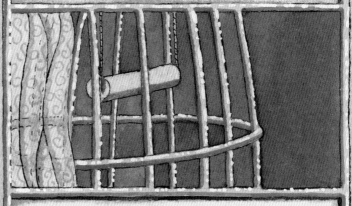

What she saw from up
there was . . .

Her
cage.

She thought she would stay
And live freely each day
Here in the park, 'neath the sky.

Then she thought she'd go back
Where there was nothing she lacked
Though she'd never be able to fly.

Have you
ever heard
Of the Little
Red Bird
Who had some
thinking to do?

Should
   she stay?

Should
   she go?

She just
   didn't know . . .

I wonder what YOU would do?